For those who draw on walls—JF

W

PENGUIN WORKSHOP
An Imprint of Penguin Random House LLC, New York

Copyright © 2020 by Jonathan Fenske. All rights reserved. Published by Penguin Workshop, an imprint of Penguin Random House LLC, New York. PENGUIN and PENGUIN WORKSHOP are trademarks of Penguin Books Ltd, and the W colophon is a registered trademark of Penguin Random House LLC. Manufactured in China.

Visit us online at www.penguinrandomhouse.com.

Library of Congress Control Number: 2019056136

ISBN 9781524793081   10 9 8 7 6 5 4 3 2 1

The art for this book was created on illustration board with #2 pencil and India ink.

After Squidnight

by Jonathan Fenske

Penguin Workshop

The sky is black.
The clouds are inky.
The salty air
is still and stinky.

You're snug in bed.
You're softly sleeping . . .

. . . while to your house
the squids are creeping.

Tick-tock.
Tick-tock.
Midnight sounds.

At the beach,
the ocean pounds.
And from the surf
a suckered hand
drags itself
onto the sand.

You dream of breezy afternoons.
The squids slide softly over dunes.

Pale artists from the ocean dark
are on their way to make their mark!

(In water, squid art
does not stay.
Inky drawings
drift away.)

So pointy heads and
arms of blue
will bring the inky
art to YOU!

In they pour,
their arms like noodles,
drawing curly, swirly doodles!

Yum! Your kitchen
looks delicious!
Through the cupboard,
over dishes.

On fridge and freezer,
leaving streaks,
dragging tentacles and beaks.

Down the hall
the dark ink dribbles.
Now your rug
is full of scribbles!

Bathroom pit stop!
Rub-a-dub.
Drawing water
in the tub.

Your room is next.
And while you snore,
the squids squeeze
underneath your door.

They draw on trucks.
They draw on dolls.
They draw on curtains,
clothes, and walls.

They draw on *you*.
But you don't care.
You do not even
know they're there!

But when you stir,
oh, how they scatter!
Their squiddy hearts
a-pitter-patter.

They wait in shadows,
big eyes blinking,
and pause their
squiddly-diddly inking . . .

. . . till all is quiet as before.
Then they ooze out
to ink some more.

They draw on doors.

They draw on hooks.

They draw on shoes,
and socks,
and books.

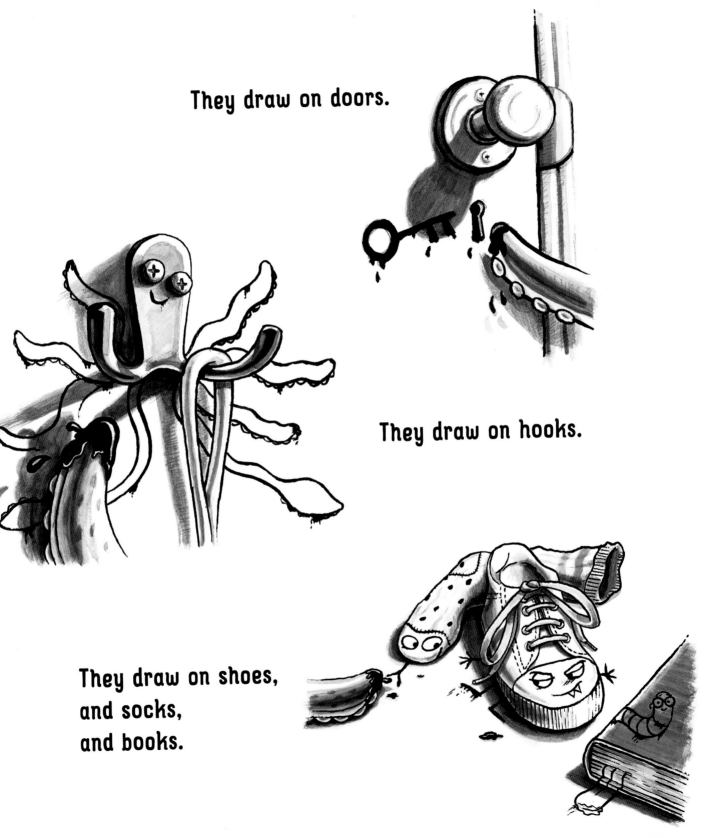

They draw until
the sunlight's glowing
lets them know
they must be going!

You wake in time
to see one still
sliding off the windowsill.

Tick-tock.
Tick-tock.
Morning sounds.

At the beach,
the ocean pounds.
And through the surf
the squids with glee
drag themselves
back to the sea.

While in your room
you blink and stare.
Your eyes adjust
to what is there.
The inky art
is *everywhere!*

Your mom and dad
are not too happy.
"Start the scrubbing!
Make it snappy!"

You try your best
to blame the squids.
But who believes
the tales of kids?

(In houses, squid art
cannot stay.
You have to wash
it all away.)

Well, not quite *all.*
For, with a smile,
in the corner,
behind a pile
of random stuff,
you save one mark,
sketched by a squid
in midnight's dark.

It's just a doodle,
nothing grand.
Left by a slimy suckered hand
whose artist's heart just had to share
with anybody who might care
that once, while you slept, unaware,
after midnight . . .

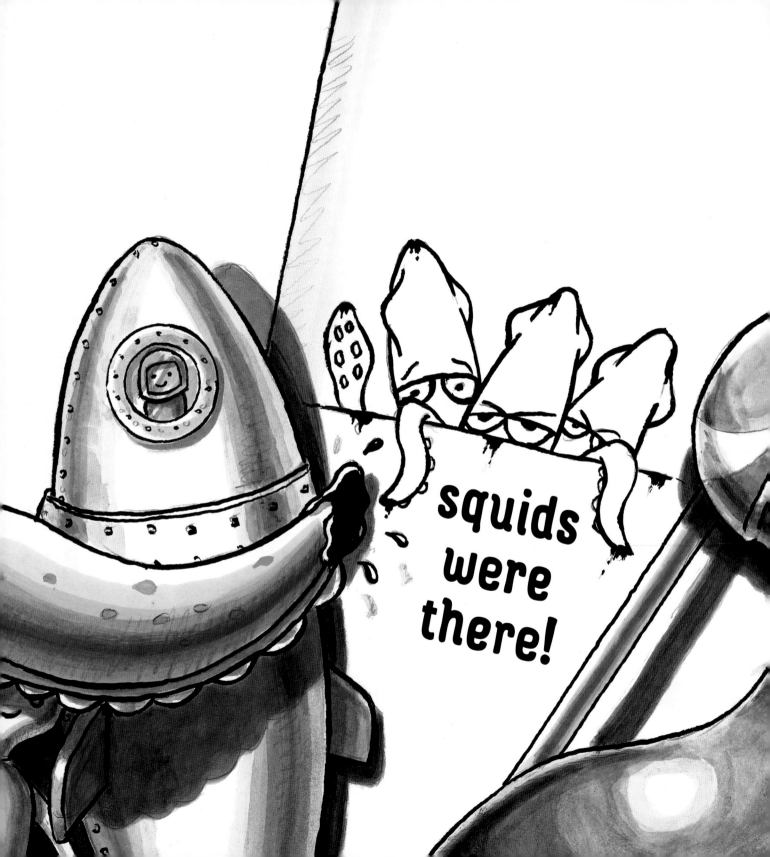

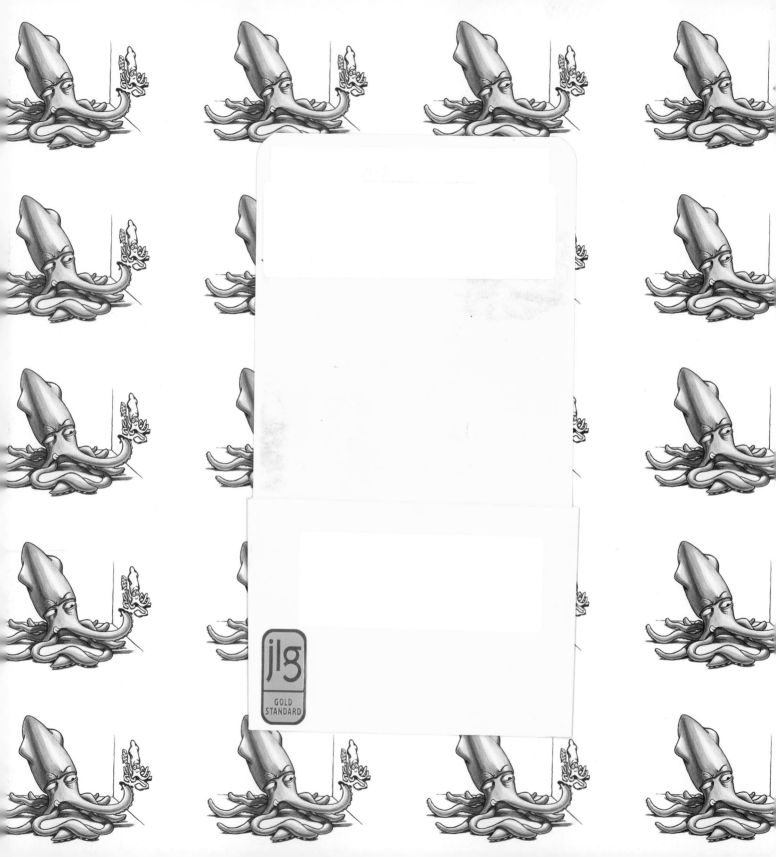